Yafi's Family

An Ethiopian Boy's Journey of Love, Loss, and Adoption

Linda Pettitt
with Sharon Darrow

Illustrations

Jan Spivey Gilchrist

Foreword

Melissa Fay Greene

AMHARIC
KIDS.COM

For Yared – son of the Amhara people, son of Ethiopia. You live your life with courage, spirit and humour. You are an inspiration to many. —LP

For Raena and Jared Prude, Grandma Jan and Grandpa Kelvin will love you forever and we will wait forever. —JSG

From the Publisher:

Yafi's Family is a work of fiction based on a common Ethiopian adoption story. We believe each adopted child's story is his or hers alone, to be held carefully until the child is old enough to own it. We hope that adopted children will connect with *Yafi's Family* in a way that validates their own special story and opens conversations to talk about it within their family. Yafi is a nickname for the Ethiopian/Hebrew name Yafet.

Many thanks to a wonderful team — all a part of the Ethiopian adoption community— who all have vested interest to get it right: the many adoptive adults, parents, and professionals who provided input; copy editor Kate Kjorlien; designer Stacy Bellward. Thank you to the Deely Family for modeling and to Samara and Caleigh Bellward for the "My Family" artwork.

Published in 2010 by Amharic Kids
Brooklyn Park, Minnesota 55445
www.armharickids.com

Text © 2010 by Amharic Kids
Illustrations © 2010 by Jan Spivey Gilchrist
All rights reserved.
Printed in South Korea
ISBN: 978-0-9797481-4-1
Library of Congress Control Number: 2010903219

AMHARIC KIDS.COM

A Message from Melissa Fay Greene

Author of *There Is No Me Without You*

Love and family are enough to help a child thrive in almost every way but this one: the human need to feel part of a deeply rooted, vibrant, and growing family tree; the desire to look like other people.

The message we relay to the children who are ours by adoption needs to be: You came from somewhere. You came from good people. You came from this spot on the globe. This is your birth-country. It is a country filled with people who look like you. Do you remember living there? Maybe you were too little to remember. But it's right there, your country, and it can be part of your life.

My husband and I have four biological children and five by adoption. Our four Ethiopian children came to us at older ages, with vivid and tender memories of their parents, their houses, their fields, and their animals. But our Bulgarian son, Jesse, placed in an orphanage as a toddler, arrived here without such precious memories. He longed for more knowledge.

Three years ago, our family flew to Ethiopia and had a chance to visit extended family members of our older Ethiopian son, Fisseha. As he was embraced, kissed, and welcomed by his step-grandmother, half-siblings, cousins, nieces, and nephews, a joyful shout went up from the crowd. It was Jesse who stood apart with tears streaming down his face. Tears of happiness for Fisseha. Tears of longing.

My husband and I hired an investigator in Bulgaria, and sent him a copy of Jesse's birth certificate, on which his birth-mother's national identification number appeared. The investigator found her, and she was thrilled to hear from us.

We couldn't all be there, as we had been at Fisseha's family reunion in Ethiopia, but we all accompanied Jesse to the computer one afternoon, and told him to expect a surprise. I opened the file. There she was: the woman of his dreams, still young, lovely, curly-haired. Jesse resembled his birth-mother like a clone. His first words were "I'm not a mystery anymore."

Later he asked me, "Are you worried that I love her more than you?" "No, sweetie, of course not!" I said, thinking *I was the one who found you in the lonely impoverished rural orphanage. I brought you home, made you our son, helped you become an all-American boy...*

Before I could get any further, he said, "Because I love you both the same."

I laughed about this later. It didn't hurt my feelings! I want my son to know that he, too, is someone's biological child.

I believe that his words—that he loves me the same as he loves a woman he glimpsed briefly in infancy—meant something like this: "I love my life as a child of our family, and I love my history and my people and my first family. I love both aspects of myself."

That is the path to wholeness.

"RRRAAAAAAH!"

"Yafi, you Big Little Lion—you scared me! Ethiopian Grandma Elsa would be very proud of that roar!"

"Do you remember that day? The day we met in Ethiopia for the first time?" asked Mom.

"I remember," said Anna and Kari.

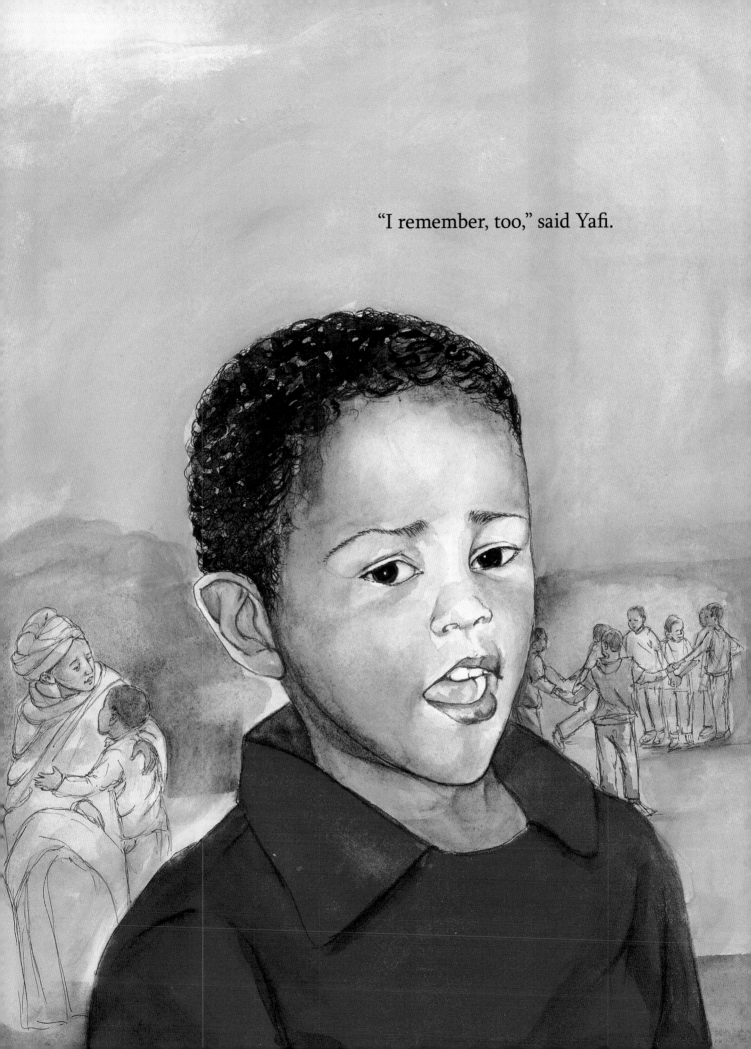

"I remember, too," said Yafi.

"At the orphanage, Biruk could roar like a lion, too. He played soccer with me, even in the rain. I got angry when he went away on the airplane with his new family. I never got to play with him again."

Dad nodded. "Biruk was your best friend. What did you do when you missed him?"

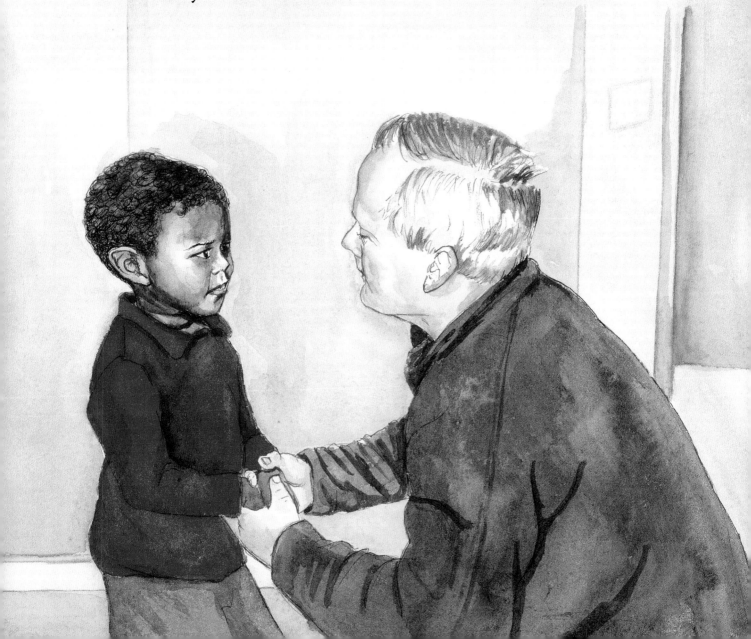

"I ran around and turned on all the lights and all the water faucets because I wanted to go on the airplane, too."

"It must have made you very sad when Biruk left to be with his new family," Mom said.

"Will Anna and Kari go away, too?"

"No, Yafi, we won't go away!" Anna said.

Mom smiled. "Dad, your sisters, you, and I will always be a family. We love you so much."

"You blew bubbles and gave me a balloon on the day we met."

Kari laughed. "I wanted to play with my new brother!"

Anna said, "We loved you as soon as we met you."

"I thought you were nice, but I couldn't understand your words. I was too scared to laugh or talk."

"It was very scary for you," Mom said. "You only spoke Amharic and they only spoke English. You were a brave boy, Yafi—brave as a lion."

"Look, there are pictures of the orphanage in my life book. Here are the nice ladies. I remember that they washed me and combed my hair on the day I met you. I liked my new clothes, but I was afraid. I was worried and missed Grandma Elsa."

"She missed you, too," Mom said. "Before you went to the orphanage in Addis Ababa, you lived in a village with Grandma Elsa. She gathered firewood every day to sell for money to buy food. She loved you very much, and she gave you all she could."

"She gave me this red sweatshirt. When I sniff it, I remember Grandma's cooking fire and the delicious taste of injera."

"I love injera!" Kari rubbed her stomach.

"And wat, too," Anna added.

"When we met Grandma Elsa, she told us that you ran and shouted and played with the other boys," Mom explained. "Everyone knew your voice."

"'Big Little Lion,' they called me, right? Because I was fierce and brave like a lion! RRAAAH!"

"Yes, Yafi, that's right," said Dad. "For a long time, your grandma and the neighbors in the village watched over you. But your grandma knew she was growing old. Sometimes she didn't have enough food to feed you or medicine to give you when you were sick."

"Grandma Elsa loved me so much that she wanted me to
have a family that could love me and take care of me."

"That's when I went to Addis Ababa to wait for you to find me."

"And we did find you!" Kari clapped her hands. "We rode on three airplanes to get all the way back to our house."

"Our whole family was waiting to meet you," Mom said. "Grandma Reid had happy tears when she hugged you for the first time. Auntie Sue brought you a toy lion and kissed you the Ethiopian way—on each cheek. Everybody was so happy you came into the family."

Anna smiled. "What did you like best when you first came home?"

"I liked breakfast, lunch, and dinner. I ate so much my tummy hurt."

"You did eat a lot at first," Mom said, "but now you know that we always have enough food for everyone."

"Sometimes I was very sad and angry."

"Yes, sometimes you were so upset that you hit me or threw things," Dad said. "I knew that you were missing Grandma Elsa. I would hold you tightly in my arms until you stopped crying and the sadness melted away."

"We don't have any pictures of my Ethiopian mother Aster because she died, right?"

"Yes, your first mother got very sick," said Dad. "When she died, your aunt took you to live with your grandma. You and Auntie traveled all night on the bus to get to Grandma Elsa's house."

"When Grandma Elsa saw you, she held you and kissed you. She loved you very much," said Mom.

"I remember her hands patting me. When I was scared in the dark, she sang songs to me."

"I think I remember Auntie and the bus, but I can't remember my first mother. When I think about her, I'm sad and I miss her. Why do I miss her when I can't remember her face?"

"When a baby is born to a mother, that baby may not remember the mother in his mind, but he can remember the love in his heart," Mom said.

Dad explained, "Families go on and on, far back in time. Your Grandma Elsa had two daughters, and she had a mother and father. She also had sisters, brothers, and grandparents. All of them are still your family."

"They are still my family, even though I'm with you every day now?"

Dad nodded. "Yes, Yafi, they are."

"And they always will be," Mom said.

"Just like we are your family," Anna and Kari hugged Yafi, "and we always will be!"

"I don't have a picture of my first mother, but I can draw one. I can draw a picture of her and Grandma Elsa. I can draw a picture with everyone in it at the same time, all my grandmas and grandpas, and you—my mom and dad and sisters."

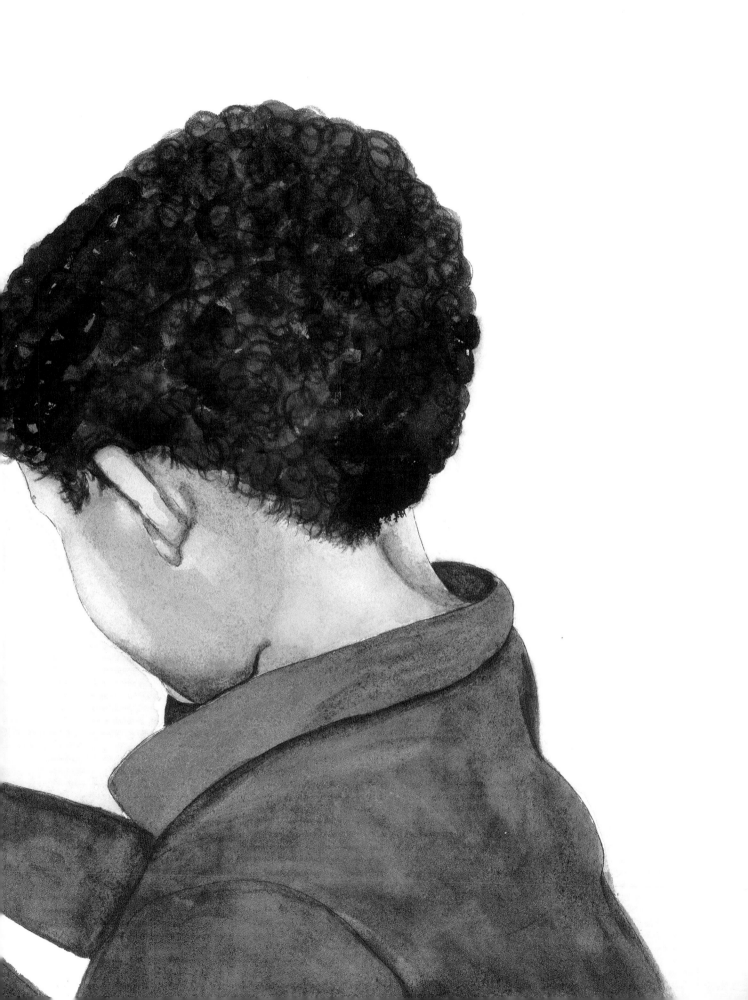